In loving memory of
"styling librarian" Debbie Alvarez,
whose passion for books lives on
—N. L.

For my wonderful mother,
whose strength inspired my own dreams,
both little & large
—M. C.

SIMON & SCHUSTER BOOKS FOR YOUNG READERS
An imprint of Simon & Schuster Children's Publishing Division
1230 Avenue of the Americas, New York, New York 10020
Text copyright © 2017 by Nina Laden • Illustrations copyright © 2017 by Melissa Castrillon
SIMON & SCHUSTER BOOKS FOR YOUNG READERS is a trademark of Simon & Schuster, Inc.
For information about special discounts for bulk purchases, please contact
Simon & Schuster Special Sales at 1-866-506-1949 or business@simonandschuster.com.
The Simon & Schuster Speakers Bureau can bring authors to your live event.
For more information or to book an event, contact the Simon & Schuster Speakers Bureau
at 1-866-248-3049 or visit our website at www.simonspeakers.com.
Book design by Lizzy Bromley • The text for this book was set in Simoncini Garamond.
The illustrations for this book were rendered in pencil and then colored digitally.
Manufactured in China • 0817 SCP • 4 6 8 10 9 7 5
Library of Congress Cataloging-in-Publication Data • Names: Laden, Nina, author. | Castrillon, Melissa, illustrator.
Title: If I had a little dream / by Nina Laden ; illustrated by Melissa Castrillon.
Description: New York : Simon & Schuster Books for Young Readers, [2017]
| "A Paula Wiseman Book." | Summary: "As a child dreams of all the things in her world that make her happy,
she realizes how fortunate she is to live in the world she does"—Provided by publisher.
Identifiers: LCCN 2016010817| ISBN 9781481439244 (hardback) | ISBN 9781481439251 (eBook)
Subjects: | CYAC: Stories in rhyme. | BISAC: JUVENILE FICTION / Bedtime & Dreams. | JUVENILE FICTION /
Social Issues / Emotions & Feelings. | JUVENILE FICTION / Stories in Verse.
Classification: LCC PZ8.3.L125 If 2017 | DDC [E]—dc23 LC record available at https://lccn.loc.gov/2016010817

If I had a little dream

By Nina Laden

Illustrated by Melissa Castrillon

A Paula Wiseman Book

Simon & Schuster Books for Young Readers

New York   London   Toronto   Sydney   New Delhi

If I had a little land,
I would name it There.
There would be my home,
be it stormy be it fair.

If I had a little house,
I would name it Love.
Love would make me happy
and protect me like a glove.

If I had a little garden,
I would name it Whole.
Whole would be filled
with roots and seeds,
and feed my heart and soul.

If I had a little pond,
I would name it Wonder.
Wonder would show me beauty
above the water and under.

If I had a little boat,
I would name it Treasure.
Treasure would make me glow inside,
more than I could measure.

If I had a little bicycle,
I would name it Wings.
Wings would take me everywhere
to see so many things.

If I had a little table,
I would name it Sweet.
Sweet would be a place to share
delicious things to eat.

If I had a little chair,
I would name it Strong.
Strong would hold me when I needed rest
until friends came along.

If I had a little dog,
I would name her Good.
Good would show me loyalty
no matter where we stood.

If I had a little cat,
I would name him Curious.

Curious would make me laugh,
and never make me furious.

If I had a little brother,
I would name him Sky.
Sky would be the air I breathe,
together we would fly.

If I had a little sister,
I would name her Song.
Song would be my lullaby
as we walked along.

If I had a little book,
I would name it Friend.
Friend would go wherever I went,
our story would never end.

If I had a little bed,
I would name it Nest.

Nest would hold my thoughts and dreams,
so they would let me rest.

If I had a little dream,
I would name it You.
You would make life magical,
where wishes do come true.